Charles M. Stebbins

Christmas Eve

and other poems

Charles M. Stebbins

Christmas Eve
and other poems

ISBN/EAN: 9783337380687

Printed in Europe, USA, Canada, Australia, Japan

Cover: Foto ©Andreas Hilbeck / pixelio.de

More available books at **www.hansebooks.com**

CHRISTMAS EVE

AND

OTHER POEMS

BY

C. MAURICE STEBBINS

SALT LAKE CITY

KELLY & COMPANY

1894

TO

The Queen of Our Home

MY MOTHER

These Poems are Lovingly Dedicated.

CONTENTS.

CHRISTMAS EVE

AND

OTHER POEMS.

CHRISTMAS EVE;

OR,

THE ALPINE SHEPHERD.

I.

There was a youth, a nursling of the mountains,
Untutored in the ways of congregated men.
His knowledge he had quaffed from the pure foun-
    tains,
And the morning streams, and flowery glen
Wherein his sheep he folded safe in pen
At eve; from the near heavens, and the light
Of day, the music of the jay and wren.
And else he knew not: neither how to write
Nor read; but in the life he lived he found delight.

II.

No mother ever watched with quickening breath
The varying struggles of his infancy:
To her the gates of life were gates of death;
No sister's sweet companionship had he
To temper and attune his childish glee.
A father's was the only care he knew;
A father's untrained knee the only knee
To which he came for knowledge.   And his view
Was narrow as the narrow valley where he grew.

III.

When spring first touched the mountains into green,
The warm sun resting on their southern side;
And birds winged lightly to a northward scene,
He, with his aged father as his guide,
Would leave the sheltered valley and abide
Thro' summer in the mountains, feeding there
The bleating sheep until late autumn-tide
Re-led them to their narrow vale to wear
Away the winter on austere and scanty fare.

IV.

And thus far from the never-ending strife
Of tho't; far from the eddying ebb and flow
Of peace and misery, of death and life;
Far from the human calm and joy that grow
From friendship; and the hopes and fears that strow
The paths of men, his spirit formed its view;
Untrained by ought less pure than the first glow
Of dawn, the water of the brook, or dew
Of evening, and the summer sky's untarnished blue.

V.

And many a day he wandered forth alone,
Beyond the limits of the meadow land,
And gained the topmost peak, the first bright throne
Of day, seeking in love to understand
The things around him, and to find a hand
Of fellowship in each least thing he saw.
And thus his simple spirit did expand
Until he felt spring up a natural awe
Toward these, his kindred, knowing not their law.

VI.

And hour by hour he stood beneath the shaggy rocks
That rise in measured rows up to the sky
That seems to softly rest its fleecy flocks
Upon them; and forgot the sensual tie
That bound him to the earth; for to his eye
Appeared more than the visible shape of things;
More than the tho't of great or small, or high
Or low. Faint echoes of retreating wings
Were these; sudden to disappear as whisperings.

VII.

To move or speak the power was not his own.
He might have prayed had he e'er heard of prayer;
Yet did his spirit worship, and the throne
At which it knelt rose thro' the trembling air;
And in this usurpation all was fair,
Loving and lovable; transcendent power
Breathed in the least of creatures everywhere.
Here littleness lived not; and every flower
That breathed added a greatness to the passing hour.

VIII.

Upraised to adoration of a Power,

Whose name is unfamiliar to his lips,

He lives, reflecting on the natural dower

Of things about him.   And the autumn slips

To spring, and spring to autumn; time strips

The mountains turn by turn of green and white,

As drop by measured drop the water drips.

The youth turned homeward on an autumn night

To find a frosty form: its spirit taken flight.

IX.

Too deep the wound for words or flow of tears!

There like a stony statue did he stand,

Whose cold impassive face defies the years

To work an equal change, or with the brand

Of dissolution mar its mien.   No hand

Were sensitive enough to thaw the frost

That bound his spirit more than to command

That to return whence it had fled; life lost

Her power; a death in life that death could not ex-

haust.

X.

Calm was the night; the moon fair on the hills;
   But calmer was despair, until day broke
At last, and melted up the frozen rills
   Of life; and then, and not till then, he spoke,
   Seeking his questionings in words to cloak:
"What is this, father, holds thy dear lips dumb?
   And is this death, whose swift and fatal stroke
   I ne'er have seen, save as it erst has come
And led away a wandering lamb to martyrdom?

XI.

"What is it that is gone, that thou canst speak
   No more? that thy fond eyes are cold and still?
   Which e'er as I came home, were wont to seek
My face. Where gone thy smile that used to fill
   My heart with rapture as I, warm or chill,
   Led homeward from the pastures; where the smile
That taught me all I know of good and ill
   And love; that I bore with me many a mile,
Hid in my heart, thro' mountain-meadow and defile?

XII.

"I tho't I loved thee well; but now I feel
  I only loved thee half; canst thou be near!
  Where is that other self of thee, the real?
  For 'tis not *thou* I see in this severe
  And rigid form; only a vision leer!
  But where the something that I cannot name:
  The vision that I see no more, nor hear?
  That sparkle in thine eyes that went and came,
That force and warmth of love that thrilled thy frame?

XIII.

"Is that, too, dead?   Can Life be lost in Death?
  And what is life and what is Death?   And where
  Is He that made them? He that fused the breath
  Into these lips? I tho't, or dreamed the air,
  One day, upon its pulsing wings did bear
  Insinuations of a Power too deep
  To be ought less than everlasting heir
  To all that is or has been: strong to keep
Eternal watch o'er all that wakes or is asleep.

XIV.

"I tho't—and could it be only a dream?
  I tho't the mountains and the air and sky,
  The trees, the birds among the trees, the stream,
  All breathed a song of ecstacy on high.
  I heard: it melted into me till I
  Became transformed; within me as without
  Was something more than human; ear and eye
  Alone performed their functions; then, a shout,
A chorus of a million voices seemed to wrap me about.

XV.

"My heart leapt in me.   Bliss and mystery!
  I loved!   And felt that I was loved and more.
  My soul grew boundless as the swelling sea,
  Encompassing the earth; I did adore!
  And grander than my own, broad as the floor
  Of heaven, streamed Love of all things—infinite!
  And seemed it must be so for evermore.
  It was about me; I was lost in it.
And must it like a dream into the darkness flit?

XVI.

"If this be so, then must all creatures weep:
  Be there no power of Love between the earth
  And man, and man and sky, then must ye keep
  With me continual mourning; and no mirth
  Forever know; but an eternal dearth
  Of joy shall be your portion, oh, ye hills,
  Ye fountains, and sweet fields and birds! and birth
  A mimic mockery.   Then must the rills
Of heaven open wide and weep for her own ills."

XVII.

He ceased; and the sad sound of his own words
  Struck maddening terror to his stricken heart.
  A spirit led him forth; and where the herds
  Had fed for many a summer day, the smart
  Of his fresh wound choking his breath, the dart
  Firm in his side, he flees by winding ways
  Familiar to his feet.   Yet does he start
  And, like some guileless, timid thing that strays,
His stealthy steps at his more stealthy shadow stays.

XVIII.

Thro' winding dells whose silence is disturbed
Alone by the swift echoes of his feet;
Or, by the bank of torrents whose uncurbed
And fitful fury to his ear seems sweet
As rest and shadow from the noon-day heat
Of summer sun, he goes; and in his brain
The fever keeps apace with the quick beat
Of his wild steps.   A hissing hurricane
Of tho't drags him on in the turmoil of its train.

XIX.

Evening came on; and thro' the solemn aisles
Of a deep wood he wandered; all the trees
Were bare; and thro' the long winding files
Of rocks and gnarled boughs the plaintive breeze
Moaned sadly, like those calm and piteous seas
That break forever on a barren strand.
Remote the wan moon rises by degrees
And sheds its cold light on the lonely land,
And on the shepherd's burning brow and chilling
    hand.

XX.

The covetous hours run on—daylight and dark—
Until upon an eve the growing gloom
Slackened the fury of his pain; the spark
That lent strength to his languid limbs gave room
To weakness—and he swooned. And like a tomb
The night-wind built with the sere leaves
A couch for him.   He sleeps; and on the loom
Of dreams, young memory with fancy weaves
About his heart her woof till it forgets to grieve.

XXI.

His father stood, of radiant face and form,
With consolation on his lips, and bade
Him leave the uncultured wild and seek a place
Among the haunts of men; then did he fade
And the first light of day faintly arrayed
The wood and mountains in reviving hope;
And daintily upon his leaf-bed played.
He rose and, in the waters that elope
From fountains, bathed his brow; then followed down
      the slope.

XXII.

In many a narrow vale and deep ravine
The slumbering echoes at his steps awoke;
And many a timid hare, scared at a mien
More innocent than her own, the frail grass broke
Beneath her anxious feet.   Of leaves of oak
Or sycamore with tender hands he made
His bed at eve; and oftentimes he spoke
To his own questionings.   At last he strayed
To a broad stream that yielded to a sinuous glade.

XXIII.

He finds an unmoored shallop by the shore,
Whose chinked and withered sides can scarce
    sustain
The weight of their decay; the fragile oar
He takes and glides out o'er the rippling plain.
Swift flows the stream; the night-wind blows amain;
The boat, like spirit-craft before the sweep
Of spirit-wind, drives on; in the blue main
Above, alternately, the sun and wan stars keep
Continual watch, beacons of an eternal deep.

XXIV.

It chanced upon the holy Christmas eve:

He sought the shelter of a lone chalet.

A father and a maiden fair receive

The way-worn guest.   In good old fashioned way

The eve is kept with rites unto the day

To come, in memory of the Christmas morn

Long centuries ago; a sacred lay

The maiden sang, and in the shepherd's lorn

And wasted heart, as the old man prayed, a hope was
    born.

XXV.

The ecstacy that he had learned from streams

And mountains, and the sun's warm light,

The expectation of his skyward dreams

Were realized: to her sublimest height

His spirit rose, and by a mystic flight

He stood once more before a sky-crowned peak,

Again loving and lovable and bright.

The cloud-caps drifting thro' the blue bespeak

That Love; in it commune all creatures, strong or
    weak.

XXVI.

And was it strange he prayed that night to die?
And was it strange the prayer, his first, was heard?
That Christmas morn rose in a cheerful sky;
Among the leafless boughs the slight wind stirred;
The morning piping of the last sweet bird
Greeted the day; a peace was in the air,
And joy o'er all; but never voice could word
The unsung joy those smiling lips declare,
Free from all touch of earth, fair as the heavens are
    fair.

EVENING ON THE OHIO.

The slow sun sinks beneath the edge
Of day, where earth and sky lie locked
In fond embrace; from peak and ledge
The last light leaps; a silent throng,
The shadows gathering steal along
In dark procession up the hills
On the Kentucky shore, and rocked
Upon a sea of waving green
They glide still on and up to flee
And mingle with the far unseen;
A fragment of infinity.

The silent river drops from rills
That lie concealed beyond the veil

Of mystery that twilight weaves
Athwart the lessening intervale
From earth to heaven, and flows in peace
More gentle than the wave of leaves
Awhile the winds for respit cease.

And now a bark majestic rides
Out of the mist; its steady light
Streams on before appareling
The waters in a calm delight.

Astern a little tremor glides
Along the surface, altering
The stillness of its placid mien.

Calmly imposing and serene
The craft unswerving passes down
Beyond the grove and harbor-bar,
The shrouded wharf and silent town,
And in the distance faints away
As faints the morning star
Or spirit to eternity.

A sacred peace reigns over all
The scene, and through the stillness come
The throbbings of the Nature-heart
With magic power to purge away
The dross of life until there fall
The fleshy curtains from the soul,
And it, released and dumb,
Forgetting how to pray,
Yet stands in adoration
Of the Power that made it.

IN CITY CREEK CANYON.

Childlike I lie upon the springing grass
That rims the road along the canyon slope,
And watch the silver-folded cloud-caps pass
In silent majesty across a sea
Of half-transparent blue: a purity
So pure that its reflection makes the earth
More free from all but truth and love,
And turns my wandering thoughts
Back to the happy day that gave me birth:
For so I count the hour that brought the dove
Of life and fused into my limbs a length
Of days sufficient to behold this hour.
To contemplate these symbols of the Power
That raised to form these ever-ancient hills

And all with purpose and with pleasure fills,
Were a sufficient prize for living.

Softly the green turf melts away
To the low edge that hems the stream.
The sprightly waters stealing in and out
Among the many windings, splash and spray
The leaves that overhang in mid-day dream;
O'erspread the stones with silken softness, shout
And sing an ever-varied melody,
And of their singing never weary; gay
And noisy in their unremitting glee
They wander on as they have done forever.
The grape of Oregon, about the spot,
Raise modestly their amorous yellow heads;
And blushing for its own deep loveliness
Amidst the grass the wild sweet William sheds
Its tender beauty, or the wild sweet pea,
The buttercup or frail forget-me-not.
The wind relenting hovers with the bee

For one short moment, bending to caress
Their dainty lips, and drunk with love of them
Loses itself amidst their fragrant fragileness,
Until a thrill vibrate each lithesome stem.

Beyond the stream a giant mass of rock
Rises far as the eye can skim the air,
And pillars up with many a massive block
Of ancient stone the vaulted arch of heaven.
Silent and stern its wrinkled mien doth stare
Hard down upon me like a Roman god;
Across its furrowed features coldly run
The characters of ages, characters
Revealing deep how Nature's works are done
By her unnumbered ministers,
That were ere day was made a name
And fashioned from the night; ere life became
On land and in the air and ageless seas;
The awful characters of Time's mysterious
And measured march through centuries;

Strange symbols that foretell the future
From the past, the story of eternity.

Calmly the day is dying, and a peace
That lives with nature only, everywhere
Is breathed by the unseen spirits of the air;
The low blue sky enriched with many a fleece
Of snowy whiteness settles round the peaks
A little closer, that with jagged arms
Support it; hushed, too, are the trembling leaves
Of aged tree and wanton weed, fit charms
For noon-day bee and evening whip-poor-will;
The flowers bend their dainty heads with cheeks
Aflush to bid farewell to the faint day;
A while the old sun smiles upon the grass
That rims the narrow marge with mellow ray,
Clambers the rocky steepness to the edge
That is the first to greet the seething dawn,
There hovers for a moment and is gone.

No voice of bird charms the entranced air,
And yet the very stillness seems to chant
An unheard requiem to the day, and there
Are strains more sweet by far than ever wind
Hath wafted to the ear from harp or lyre
Touched by a human.hand; a visitant
Unseen bears them upon her trembling wings
Straight from the ethereal lute of Silence, shrined
In twilight shades of wooded aisle and spire;
And audible to the inward ear alone,
She breathes her deep mute music, and the end
And the beginning into one strain blend:
Which is life, love and immortality.

THE SKY SEEMS DESOLATE.

The sky seems desolate to-day;
The birds that fly across the grey
An evil portent seem to bring
To me, with heavy-flapping wing;
The piping of the wren is wrought
With melancholy; winds have caught
The plaintive pulsings of the sea;
Even the overbrimming glee
Of brook and spring is blent
With murmurings of discontent;
The sun, the old untiring sun,
Seems weary of the task begun
This morn, and toils across the sky
As if his pathway were too high,

Or he had lost a friend,
Or sought a too far-distant end.
Yet Sergius sings with keen delight;
To him the day is pure and bright
As ever day might be;
A gaysome minstrelsy
Reigns over all; the very streets
Are redolent with flowery sweets,
Like fields in May.
A happy chance befell
Him yesterday;
I bade a hope farewell.

COULD I BUT SING.

Could I but sing as the old earth has sung
For centuries; could I but catch among
Her wild ethereal melodies one note
Of minor chord, of those that ceaseless float
Thro' forest-aisle and evening-tinctured sky,
Or feel the pathos of a wave's deep sigh,
Or reach one wonder of a cloudlet's fold,
One wonder of the tiny waves of gold
That float above the far horizon's rim
And fill the world up to its shelving brim,
One growing wonder of the smallest flower
That e'er lent fragrance to a summer bower;
Could I but catch one woodland strain
From the wild wind that wanders thro' the plain,

With sweetest music for a lover's ear,
From dawning till the closing year,
Or tell one beauty of the leaf of grass
That bends to hear the mountain waters pass;
Thro' time the liquidy should roll along
And teach mankind the potency of song.

IN HARVEST TIME.

It was a day in harvest-time,
And as I wandered thro' the fields
Of yellow grain, some softly waved
Beneath the mild caresses of the wind;
Some was in fresh lain swathes;
And some lay bound in mellow sheaves.
Oh, the mysterious work of time!
Oh, the creative Love in sun!
Oh, the enlivening Power in rain!
Only a few short months ago
The seeds were scattered on the ground;
The little blades sprang to the light
And grew, perfected in the ear;
And now the harvest fully ripe!

I tho't and wandered on once more,
And found stretched out to rest
Upon the prostrate grain, his scythe close by,
The mower spent with heat and toil.
His face was thin and wrinkled much,
Grey were his hair and beard with age.
Weary with age and toil, I tho't,
And at the tho't my heart grew sad.
"To live on this fair earth is sweet,
And youth is full of happiness,
Then why must we each one grow old?"
Into the far-off skies I cried.
My eyes fell on the ripened grain,
And read reply: because the harvest
Is better than the growing grain.

OLIVER WENDELL HOLMES.

"Leaving thine outgrown shell by life's unresting sea."
—*Chambered Nautilus.*

Weep, weep! yet wherefore should we weep?
Why weep that yonder bark be quit?
For such a voyager unfit,
To bear him longer o'er the deep.

Why weep that with a sturdy oar
A long successful voyage is past,
And he has beached his boat at last
Beyond the breakers, safe on shore.

Mid storm or calm, no flood-tide swells
Upon the farther shore of life
But into port, with deathless strife,
Some wandering voyager impels.

With steady arm and eye serene,
Not every sailor steers his bark,
With one clear star to quell the dark
And guide him through the strange demesne.

With tattered sail or splintered mast
Or with a piece of broken oar,
Some struggling in the waves gain shore.
With pain; but all put in at last.

Then cease lament, for nought has failed:
He lives beyond the reach of fate;
And nought lies lone and desolate
Save the frail craft in which he sailed.

AUTUMN NOTES.

Oh fair, oh sweet, oh lovely autumn·time !
To clothe thy beauties in a fitting rhyme
Were not so frail a task: for never spring
With all the mirth that birds and bushes bring
Was half so fair in dress, or form, or tho't as thee:
In love or minstrelsy.

No fragile buds are bursting in the copse,
No green clothes the rough mountain tops;
But crowned with might and majesty they rise
In fellowship with closer bending skies.
The sun, no longer fierce, shines with a mellow ray,
More friendly than in May.

The life they live more deeply to be seen
Than when 'tis mantled in deceptive green,
That thrills from barren peak to flowery glen,
Reveals relationship 'twixt them and men:
A bond to bind us to the earth that we have trod,
And lift us unto God.

The brook runs purer o'er its rocky bed,
Past the wild coverts whence the birds have fled;
And calmly its contented chatter steals
More faint and far, in sweeter, swifter peals,
Unmixed with ought impure, and sinks into the soul.
Fleet as the waters roll.

No sullen visions of a wasted life,
No plaintive whisperings of a fruitless strife,
As one has lately muttered in my ear,
And no insinuations of a fear
That life may ever end in death my heart receives
From the discolored leaves.

All things breathe faith in immortality:
In Love that ever was and ever is to be.
It flows from every song or sound that brakes,
And fruitful melodies that silence wakes;
And life and death, and tho't, and sound and silence
blend
In one eternal trend.

SONG OF AUTUMN.

I come on the wings of the South-wind;
　On the wings of the South and East;
I tarry in forest and meadow,
　And spread out my harvest-feast.

I am Life, I am Death, and Harvest,
　The Soul of the Summer and Spring,
The end of their budding and blooming,
　Of the Months and the Years I am King.

My coffers are full; I give freely
　To the strong and the weak as well:
To man, and the birds of the meadow,
　The squirrel and fox in the dell.

For mine are the barley and wheat fields,
  The apples of red and green,
The chestnuts of brown on the hilltops,
  The fields of corn between.

For me grapes in purple clusters
  Hang low on the rustic vine;
And orchards of pears and peaches
  Their garlanded heads incline.

I bring unto all a blessing
  From inland lake to the sea;
I strew the highlands with plenty,
  The valleys I fill with glee.

No dingle may lie so hidden
  That *I* do not spy it out,
And fill with the wealth of my treasures
  Each distant and secret redoubt.

For all countries are my dominions,
   From pole to equator and pole;
And my coursers are swift as the light'nings
   To bear me from goal to goal.

My thanks are often but curses,
   Yet still do I wander on;
And gladly bestow my bounties
   Till my wealth is vanished and gone;

Then I flee on the wings of the North-wind,
   On the wings of the North and West;
And leave to the keeping of Winter
   The lands that I have blest. ·

SOWN.

The fruit-laden winds of the autumn blew
And two small seeds to a flower-plot threw,
Then buried them deep on the lifeless ground
With all the dead leaves and stems to be found.

Then the hoar-frost came and the sleet and snow,
And over the garden did reveling go;
But the seeds slept on in their rose-leaf bed
Until the winter was up and fled,

And then they sprang forth in the morning light,
And drank their fill from the tears of night,
Till their young leaves swelled with the breath of
     spring
As it filled the world in its wandering.

One of them grew enriched with the dower
And promise of being a perfect flower,
Enjoying the blessings it each day won
From the gentle rain and the patient sun.

The petals blew open at last to the air
Laying its beautiful breast all bare,
Upholding its love to each panting breeze
That lingered to whisper its tender pleas.

Not a soul ever passed the flower by
But felt the joy of its presence nigh.
And the bees that lodged on its slender tips
Instilled the dew from its lovely lips.

But there entered the garden a hand one day.
And plucked the blossoms and bore them away
To cheer with their beauty and sweet perfume
The weary hours of a sick child's room.

But others sprang up in the vacant place
And filled it full with their radiant grace;
Yet the plant gave cheerfully all it had
To make the heart of the young child glad.

A blessing to earth was this little flower,
So pure and so gentle, so great in its power,
As long as the summer gave to it breath,
And then it folded its leaves in death.

But, alas, the other and comlier seed
Developed to be but an ugly weed;
All cumbrous and dank and worthless and tall,
It thrust out its branches unloved of all.

It drank up the rain and the morning dew,
And the sunshine out of the heavens blue;
Yet it only cumbered the ground where it stood,
Ill-shapen and poisonous, void of all good.

LOVE LIES A-COLD.

In the cool garden closes,
  Where summer and care
  Have wrought beauty so rare;
Where the perfume of roses
  Is spent on the air;
  With a reticent glare,
The soft sunshine reposes
  On the bright-blown flowers
  For hours upon hours.

Not a breath stirs the willows,
  That border the stream,
  From their mid-day dream;
And the slow swelling billows

Are gathering each beam
From the sun, with a gleam
On the sea as it pillows
The shallops and skiffs
Beyond the clear cliffs.

But the day shall shiver
And die ere a sound
Stir a leaf from the ground,
Or a voice wake a quiver
From the park to the mound,
Save the baying hound
Or the tremulous river;
For Love lies a-cold
In the castle old.

From the night till the morning,
From morning till night,
When the last lonesome light
Fills the sky with its warning

Of day's damask flight,
Neither lady nor knight,
The frail flowers scorning,
Shall pluck a red rose
From the garden's close.

And the bright breath of summer
Shall pass into fall;
And the confident call
Of the busy-winged hummer
Shall cease from the wall
Where the woodbines crawl:
Nor the steps of the comer
Of the now dead days
Shall quicken the ways.

The grey gates shall crumble
And turn into sand,
But never a hand
Or a finger shall humble

Itself to withstand
The decay, till it brand
All the walls, and they tumble
And turn into clay,
For year and for day.

And the flowers, forsaken,
May wither and die:
For the wind shall sigh,
And the branches be shaken;
But never a cry,
Or a tear to the eye,
Shall it startle or waken:
For Love lies a-cold
In the castle old.

So the years shall wither
By months and by days,
From Mays unto Mays;
And the sails flee thither,

O'er the watery ways,
From yonder bleak bays,
Where the moon and with her
The timid stars shine
On the barren sea-brine;

And from father this story
Of love to the son
Shall descend; and none
Shall forget the old glory,
Till the sand be run
From his glass; or the sun
And the stars grow hoary,
And be not the lights
Of the days and nights.

But the castle and garden
Of days then long dead,
Awhile love was shed
O'er the walls that guard on

The west, shall be wed
To waste, and each bed
To a stone shall harden:
For Love lies a-cold
In the castle old.

AT EVEN-TIDE.

The western sky in crimson dyed
   Sinks softly o'er the earth's dark breast,
   Shedding abroad a lingering rest,
         At even-tide.

The shadows climb the mountain-side
   One after one with solemn pace,
   As if aspiring into space,
         At even-tide.

How listlessly the light boats glide
   Reflected in the gleaming mere,
   While the lone heron hovers near,
         At even-tide.

And ere the vesper chimes have died
    The monk's low hymn, the chant, the prayer,
    Rise trembling on the darkening air,
            At even-tide.

The sated flocks lie down beside
    The fold, and their meek spirits blend
    With nature in the day's mild end,
            At even-tide.

The brown bright thrushes sing and hide;
    A sigh is echoed from the hill;
    A star shines out and all is still,
            At even-tide.

PEGNO D'AFFETTO.

I lay these roses at thy feet, love,
   Content to lay them there
If only you may breathe their sweet, love,
   Or place one in your hair.

But crush and bruise them if you will, love,
   Their fragrance is more sweet,
And bruised and broken they will still, love,
   Lie pleading at thy feet.

And so I freely lay this heart, love,
   A suppliant at thy feet,
But if to crush it be your part, love,
   'Twill only plead more sweet.

TIME.

The clock of time has sounded
   From the belfry-tower of space:
Its silent echoes falling,
   Steal on with a mystic pace.

The clock ticks on, on ever
   The same quaint tick as before,
And the leaves of the future rustle
   As they have done of yore.

The future is but the present,
   The present is but the past,
And *that* lies in the boundless
   Always to live and last.

THE POET'S PRAYER.

O kindly Nature, thou who sovereign art
   And kindred of my being, bend to resign
   One jealous-guarded mystery of thine:
One simple token of thy favor dart
Amidst the longings of a wistful heart;
   O let me worship at thy inmost shrine
   Until I feel thy holy life is mine
And find in thee a glorious counterpart:
Then shall my minstrelsy be ever free,
   And all unheard I'll sing in solitude
The rural music of simplicity,
And mingle my faint pipings with the stream
   That chatters by, content if understood
By thee and thine, unenvious of esteem.

SONNET.

Over this brink the waters ever pour
From healthy morn unto thoughtful eve,
And through the lingering night till daybreak weave
Again the sun-light on the grassy shore,
In many a daring stream of swollen store,
Where a small lake bounds eager to receive
Them to its breast; and still without reprieve
It whispers, and the caverns echo: *more*.
So, tender Nature, do I long for thee;
Although a thousand varied streams of truth
I ever drank of thee from my first youth,
From brook and cliff, from cloud and cerul sea,
Still is my thirst too deep to satisfy
And, thus, too deep it shall be till I die.

EXPECTATION.

Sometimes I've seen from some far-distant hill,
   Appareled in the glory of the dawn
   When first she smiles upon the dripping lawn,
A little stream drop down with many a rill
Of such delicious sparkle that a thrill
   Transfixed my being, and ere the spell had gone
   Bound out beneath my feet and on where yawn
The mighty deeps that nought can drain or fill.
So I have dreamed ethereal dreams
   Of what should be upon a distant day,
The future lending color to the schemes,
   But soon, too soon, the visions died away—
A present unfulfilled, and then, at last,
Faint murmurs on the ocean of the past.